MM/YY _3|19_

$$ _16.99_

Vend. _B&T_

Series # _____

#/Discs _____

(J) YA   A   PAR

REF   PRO   OTH

_____ _

Goodwin Library
422 Main St.
Farmington NH
03835
603.755.2944

_____ _

Patron Initials here

Good Night, Library

Written by Denise Brennan-Nelson

Illustrated by Marco Bucci

Good night, library;
Darkness falls.
It's sleepy time
For these great walls.

Good night, library.
You must be tired
From all the learning
You've inspired.

Good night, words
And chapter books.
Good night, reading
In cozy nooks.

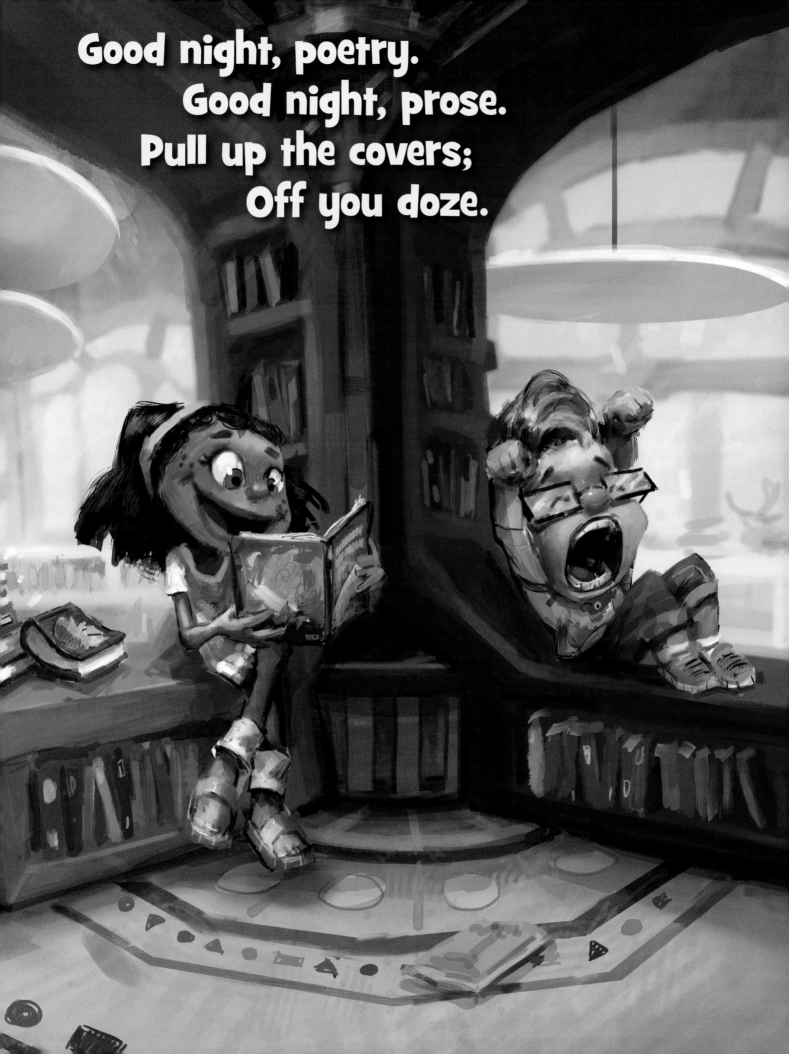

Good night, characters.
Close your pages.
Good night, plots
And puppet stages.

Good night, Goldilocks
And sleepy bears.

Good night, story time
And carpet squares.

Good night, board games,
Crafts, and art.

Good night, computer
And filing cart.

Good night, folktales
And Little Red.

Good night, Wolf
In Grandma's bed.

Good night, maps,
And atlas, too.

Good night, comics,
Old and new.

Good night, benches.
Good night, chairs.
No more climbing—
Good night, stairs.

Good night, librarian;
It's time to close.

Now all your books
Are tucked in tight.

Good night, library.
Good night, good night!

To my favorite librarian, Aunt Carolyn.

—Denise

*This book is for anyone who wants to grow up
telling stories and painting pictures.*

—Marco

Text Copyright © 2019 Denise Brennan-Nelson
Illustration Copyright © 2019 Marco Bucci
Design Copyright © 2019 Sleeping Bear Press

Sleeping Bear Press®
2395 South Huron Parkway, Suite 200
Ann Arbor, MI 48104
www.sleepingbearpress.com

Printed and bound in the United States.

10 9 8 7 6 5 4 3 2 1

Library of Congress Cataloging-in-Publication Data

Names: Brennan-Nelson, Denise, author. | Bucci, Marco, illustrator.
Title: Good night, library / written by Denise Brennan-Nelson ; illustrated
by Marco Bucci.
Description: Ann Arbor, MI : Sleeping Bear Press, [2019] | Summary:
Illustrations and simple text offer a good night to the library and its inhabitants—
including puppet shows, comics, and the books tucked safely on their shelves.
Identifiers: LCCN 2018037508 | ISBN 9781585364060 (hardcover)
Subjects: | CYAC: Stories in rhyme. | Libraries—Fiction. | Bedtime—Fiction.
Classification: LCC PZ8.3.B7457 Gn 2019 | DDC [E]—dc23
LC record available at https://lccn.loc.gov/2018037508